Why Can't I Fly?

by
Rita Golden Gelman

Pictures by
Jack Kent

SCHOLASTIC INC.

New York • Toronto • London • Auckland • Sydney

ISBN 0-590-40506-3

Text copyright © 1976 by Rita Golden Gelman.
Illustrations copyright © 1976 by Jack Kent.
All rights reserved. Published by Scholastic Inc.
HELLO READER (logo) is a trademark of Scholastic Inc.

25 24 23 22 21 20   9/9 0 1 2/0

Printed in the U.S.A.   23

To Mitchell

"I can run," Minnie said,

"I can jump up so high."

I can swing.

I can hang.

I can climb to the sky.

But somebody tell me, please.

WHY CAN'T I FLY?"

"Hmm! Let me see.

Let me think . . .

I know why!

It's those things on your feet.

Those feet-things can't fly.

Take them off.

Take them off.

Then climb way up high.

Without things on your feet
I am sure you will fly.
Goodbye."

11

Minnie climbed in her feet.

She climbed to the top.

And she said,

"I can fly,

I can fly,

I can . . .

flop.''

"Oh no!

What a mess.

That's not right.

That's all wrong.

You don't fly with your feet.

You fly with a song.

I sing all the time.

I sing low.

I sing high.

Go back up and sing

Because songs make you fly.

Goodbye."

So up Minnie went

And she sang from the top,

"I can fly,

I can fly,

I can fly,

I can . . .

flop.''

"No, that's not right.

Can't you tell?

Can't you see?

If you want to fly

You need spots like me.

Let me spot you with red.

Let me spot you with black.

On your tail, on your head,

On your ears, on your back.

Now you have spots.

You will sail through the sky.

No worry at all,

Because spots make you fly.

Goodbye.''

And so with her spots
Minnie climbed to the top.

And she said,

"I can fly,

I can fly,

I can . . .

flop.''

"Oh no, no!

No, no, no!

That's not how you do it.

It's feathers you need.

Yes, that's all there is to it.

Let me glue you all up.

Then before you get dry,

Just roll in those feathers.

And then you will fly.

Goodbye.''

So she rolled in the feathers.

And she climbed to the top.

And she said,

"I can fly,

I can fly,

I can . . .

flop.''

"It isn't your feet,
And it isn't the song.
It isn't the feathers.
Oh no, they are wrong.

And it isn't — it isn't —

Those red and black things!

If you want to fly,

You have to have wings.

We will make some right now.
We can if we try.

And when you have wings,

I am sure you will fly.

Goodbye."

So she put on her wings.

And she went to the top.

And she said,

"I can fly.

I can fly.

I can . . .

flop.''

"It's no use.

I give up.

I won't fly.

I will climb."

"You WILL fly!
Go up in that tree
one more time."

"All right," Minnie said.

"But it's my last try."

And she said,

"I can fly.

I can fly . . .

I CAN FLY !"

"Goodbye."